S. A. Trimby first trained as a nursery nurse before becoming a primary school teacher, which she has now been for twenty years. She has become a phonics specialist over this time and developed a passion for teaching literacy, particularly reading. She has enjoyed reading many stories since childhood through to her adult teaching life. She is delighted to present her first fairy story for young children.

One Magical Night in the Enchanted Woods

S. A. Trimby

AUSTIN MACAULEY PUBLISHERS™

LONDON • CAMBRIDGE • NEW YORK • SHARJAH

A CIP catalogue record for this title is available from the British Library.

ISBN 9781528997676 (Paperback)
ISBN 9781528997683 (ePub e-book)

www.austinmacauley.com

First Published 2022
Austin Macauley Publishers Ltd®
1 Canada Square
Canary Wharf
London
E14 5AA

I dedicate this book to all the imaginative young readers, wherever they may be.

I would like to thank Austin Macauley Publishers for giving me the chance to see my work in print.

I would particularly like to thank my partner, Ash, for believing in me and my writing. Also, my parents for supporting me to achieve my dream.

I ventured into the **woods** one day,
I thought it would be the best place to play.

The tallest of **trees**, a perfect den,
I tiptoed in, closed my eyes and counted to ten.

What was that? I heard a sound,
Was it something falling to the ground?

There it was, I heard it again.
What was it? I had to know and then,

My eyes focused, adjusted to the light,
I could just make out something that was glowing and white.

I crept towards the shimmering glow,
I knew I had to be silent, so I went cautiously slow.

A twig snapped under my feet,
I stopped, stood still, my heart missing a beat.

I continued my journey, my heart beating fast,
I wondered what I would find, then at last,

What was this? What could I see?
My sight was obscured by a tall, twisted tree.

I crept up behind the old gnarled tree,
I knew that I just had to see.

I peered around and saw a strange glow,

It was a **tiny orb**, as white as snow!

It shimmered in the fading sunlight,
I couldn't believe my eyes, was this right?

It looked like the tiniest little boy,

He flitted around like a magical to

But wait, he wasn't on the ground,
He was in the air gliding, not making a sound.

I looked closer, I'm sure the boy had tiny **wings,**
I started to imagine all kinds of things.

Where did he come from? What was his name?
After this, I knew things would never be the same.

He flew silently from tree to tree;
I knew that he hadn't spotted me.

8

Was he alone? Did he have a friend?
I didn't want this dream to end!

I followed him deeper into the **wood**,
I really didn't know if I should!

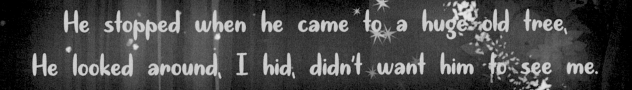

He stopped when he came to a huge old tree,
He looked around, I hid, didn't want him to see me.

Could I see a tiny wooden door?
I wondered what or who it was for.

I soon found out, he knocked on the door,
A tiny girl answered it, I'm sure!

He flew inside, what was in there?
I had to see; I just didn't care!

I tiptoed over to the tree,
There was a tiny window there, you see.

Inside was a **tiny, perfect house,**
Just the right size for a little field mouse!

It had dainty chairs and a table to match,
At first, I thought there must be a catch!

The tiny boy and girl were having a drink,
And now I really started to think.

Were they **Fairies?** Could they talk?
Did they just fly or could they walk?

Did I dare to knock on the door?
I held my breath and tapped; they
must have heard me for sure.

There was a flustered sound as things moved inside,
The tiny girl and boy just decided to hide.

After a while they appeared at the door
I waved my hand as they seemed unsure.

held out my hand, the girl flew onto my palm,
All at once everything seemed incredibly calm.

It felt like time had stopped still for me,
Like I was floating around and free.

The boy came out bringing a **drink**,

I took a tiny sip and started to **shrink**.

14

I became the same size as the tiny girl,
Something strange was happening,
it was my wings beginning to unfurl!

The girl whispered and told me that they lived in the tree,
But they often went on exciting journeys, you see!

They asked if I would like to try and fly,
But suddenly, I felt incredibly shy.

We flew through the woods but stayed quite low,
As at first, I was painfully slow.

As I improved, we went further away
And I really just have to say,

It was so exhilarating, you see,
Flying on my own, I felt so free!

I flapped my wings and started to fly;
The wind whipped my hair as the world flew by.

I was a fairy; I had wings,

That meant I could do all kinds of things!

I flitted around and took in the amazing view;
I wish that you could see it too!

Then it started getting cold in the dark night air,
How long had we been up there?

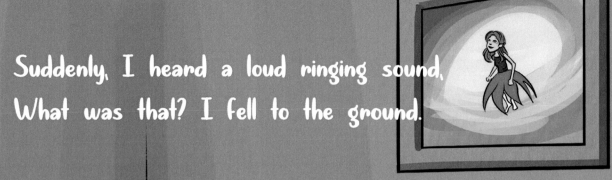

Suddenly, I heard a loud ringing sound,
What was that? I fell to the ground.

Slowly, I started to stir, I was in my own bed,
I was very confused as I rubbed my head.

I opened my eyes; how could this be?
It was the alarm clock going off, you see!

So what was that? Was it just a dream?
But things aren't always as they seem.

I jumped out of bed, looked in my pocket,
And there it was, the tiny gold locket.

The fairy girl had given it to me,
So I would never forget the night I was free;

Who knows where my next venture
will be?

I do hope that you will
come and join me.